THE RETURN OF THE BUFFALOES

THE RETURN OF THE BUFFALOES

a Plains Indian story
about famine
and renewal of the Earth
told and illustrated
by Paul Goble

NATIONAL
GEOGRAPHIC
SOCIETY

Washington, D.C.

The illustrations are in India ink and watercolor, on Oram and Robinson Limited, Waltham Cross, England, watercolor boards. Reproduced in combined line and halftone. Book designed by Paul Goble.

Printed and bound in the United States.
First edition
10 9 8 7 6 5 4 3 2 1

Library of Congress ℭℙ Data
Goble, Paul.
    The return of the buffaloes : a Plains Indian story about famine and renewal of the earth / told and illustrated by Paul Goble ; prepared by the Book Division, National Geographic Society. — 1st ed.
        p. cm.
    Summary: Based on a Lakota myth in which a mysterious woman returns the buffalo and the other animals to the Indian people.
    ISBN 0-7922-2714-X
    1. Indians of North America—Great Plains—Folklore. 2. Indians of North America—Great Plains—Food—Juvenile literature 3. Famines—Great Plains—History—Juvenile literature. [1. Teton Indians—Folklore. 2. Indians of North America—Great Plains—Folklore. 3. Folklore—Great Plains.] I. Title.
E78.G73G615 1996
398.2'090108997—dc20

94-27873

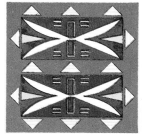

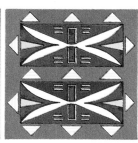

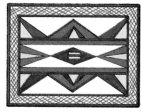

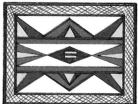

REFERENCES: Amos Bad Heart Bull and Helen H. Blish, *A Pictographic History of the Oglala Sioux,* University of Nebraska Press, Lincoln, 1967, p. 289. J. Owen Dorsey, *A Study of Siouan Cults,* Eleventh Annual Report of the Bureau of American Ethnology, Smithsonian Institution, Washington, D.C., 1889, p. 476. James LaPointe, *Legends of the Lakota,* The Indian Historian Press, San Francisco, 1976, p. 79. Alice Marriott and Carol Rachlin, *American Indian Mythology,* Thomas Y. Crowell, New York, 1968, p. 138. Emerson N. Matson, *Legends of the Great Chiefs,* Storypole Press, Tacoma, 1972, p. 39. Tom McHugh, *The Time of the Buffalo,* Alfred A. Knopf, New York, 1972, p. 133. Marie L . McLaughlin, *Myths and Legends of the Sioux,* Bismarck, 1916, p. 104. Vivien One Feather, *Ehanni Ohunkakan,* Red Cloud Indian School, Pine Ridge, 1974, p. 153. R.D. Theisz, *Buckskin Tokens—Contemporary Oral Narratives of the Lakota,* Sinte Gleska College, Rosebud, 1975, p. 12. James R. Walker, *Lakota Belief and Ritual,* University of Nebraska Press, Lincoln, 1980, pp. 124, 144. *Wind Cave National Park, South Dakota,* National Park Service Handbook 104, U.S. Dept. of the Interior, Washington, D.C., 1979, p. 31.
PARFLECHES: Kenneth Canfield, *Parfleche,* Canfield Gallery, Santa Fe, 1983. Kansas City Art Institute, *Native American Parfleche—A Tradition of Abstract Painting,* Kansas City, 1984. Mable Morrow, *Indian Rawhide—An American Folk Art,* University of Oklahoma Press, Norman, 1975. Gaylord Torrence, *The American Indian Parfleche—A Tradition of Abstract Painting,* Des Moines Art Center, Des Moines, 1994.
THANK YOU: Ron Terry, Chief of Interpretation, Wind Cave National Park, Black Hills, South Dakota.
Penny Starr, Larrry Frederick, Clarissa Reid, Kim Morgen of the National Park Service.
Kenneth Canfield for photographs and information on parfleches.

Wakan Tanka cajeyata

for Dennis Carter

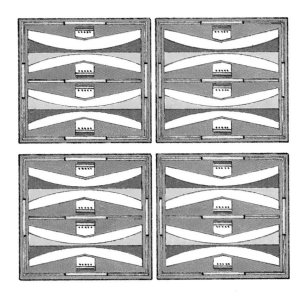

AUTHOR'S NOTE:

For nomadic peoples who lived on the High Plains, the buffalo was a gift from the Great Spirit, and supplied almost everything material which they needed: their flesh to eat, robes to wear, skins to cover tipis, and dung to burn on the largely treeless plains. This wonderful relationship had always existed, but occasionally the herds wandered to faraway places, and then there was terrible famine. It is a theme which appears again and again in the mythology.

It is told that at times of great need a beautiful and mysterious woman brings back the buffalo. She is one of the Buffalo People transformed into a woman, sent by her Buffalo Nation to tell humankind of their great love and the gift of themselves so that people can live. Here she appears to two young men who are searching for the buffalo herds. She tells them, "I will feed your people," and the story relates that she brought the buffaloes out of Wind Cave in the Black Hills of South Dakota.

I have taken this Lakota myth as the basis for this book because I have lived for many years in the Black Hills, and have heard Lakota people refer to it. I have felt the magical breath of air at Wind Cave's "Breathing Hole," **Washun Niya**, so called because of the air which rushes in or out through the hole in the rock at times of change in barometric pressure. Lakota tradition tells that it is the breath of the myriads of the Buffalo People, deep down inside the Earth, waiting for the holy woman to let them out to replenish the Earth. In your mind's eye you see them surging up out of the cave, rushing down the ravines in clouds of dust and thunder of hooves, and out of the hills through the "Doorway of the Buffaloes," **Pte Tatiopa**, which is called Buffalo Gap on today's maps.

The worlds of nature and the spirits are full of wonders and miracles, and this is mirrored in the mythology. We are told that in times of need the sacred woman will return again and again throughout time to renew the Earth. Parables like these germinated on this continent and must have been told for many thousands of years, helping to guide people to live in a most wonderful state of unselfish give-and-take with Creation. Although this story is linked with Wind Cave, the ideas are by no means limited to that place. Readers should think of the story in relation to any hill or mountain, spring or cave which they know well, and which they sense is right. Renewal of the Earth starts in our hearts, and so it can take place anywhere.

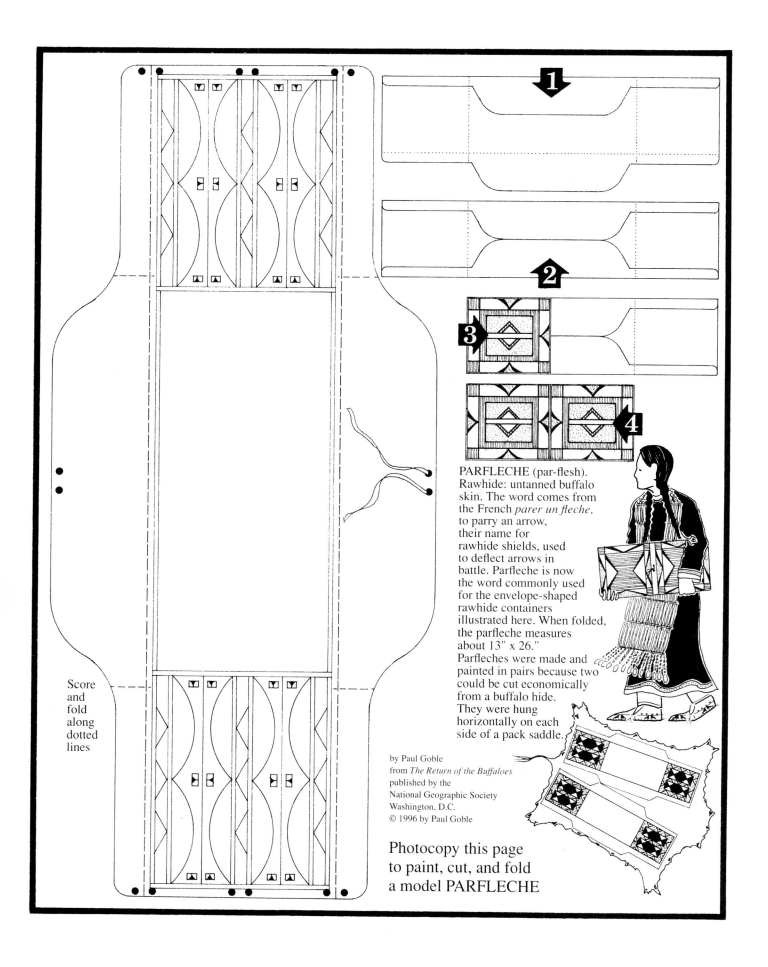

Score
and
fold
along
dotted
lines

PARFLECHE (par-flesh).
Rawhide: untanned buffalo
skin. The word comes from
the French *parer un fleche,*
to parry an arrow,
their name for
rawhide shields, used
to deflect arrows in
battle. Parfleche is now
the word commonly used
for the envelope-shaped
rawhide containers
illustrated here. When folded,
the parfleche measures
about 13" x 26."
Parfleches were made and
painted in pairs because two
could be cut economically
from a buffalo hide.
They were hung
horizontally on each
side of a pack saddle.

by Paul Goble
from *The Return of the Buffaloes*
published by the
National Geographic Society
Washington, D.C.
© 1996 by Paul Goble

Photocopy this page
to paint, cut, and fold
a model PARFLECHE

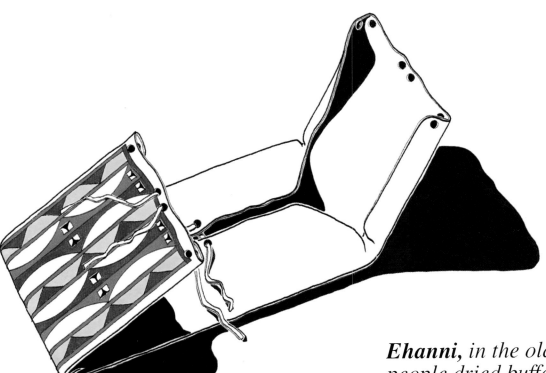

The geometric designs which decorate the book are copies of parfleche designs painted by women between about 1875 and 1930. Most of the designs are Lakota, with a few from their Arapaho and Cheyenne friends.

Ehanni, *in the old days, people dried buffalo meat in the sun to preserve it. They ate this during the winter when it was too cold to go out, or when the hunters could not find fresh meat. Great quantities of dried buffalo meat were stored in large folded rawhide cases, rather like envelopes, called parfleches. Bulging parfleches made a family feel secure against hunger.*

If there came a time when there was nothing left to eat, the parfleches empty, then everyone went hungry. They starved.

The old people used to say that because birds and animals give their lives so we can eat, we give thanks for food. They told this story:

Spring had come, but the buffaloes had not returned, and grass was even growing in the paths they always used.

The winter supplies of dried meat had all been eaten. The parfleches were empty. Everyone was hungry and the children were too weak to go out and play any longer. Women broke up old bones to boil with leaves and roots for soup. The people were starving.

"Where have the buffaloes gone?" everyone asked. Nobody knew. Even the deer and elk were nowhere to be found. Day after day hunters went out searching. People waited, yet at evening the hunters always came back empty-handed.

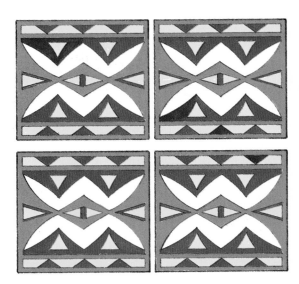

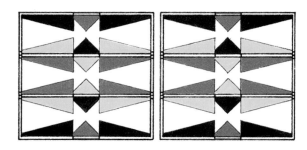

Young men kept a lookout on the hilltops, always hoping to see the buffalo herds.

People who had spoken with animals in their dreams gathered at the center of the camp. Deer and Elk and Buffalo Dreamers made ceremonies and danced, calling the animals to come back. People watched, and joined in with their thoughts, knowing that the mystic dreamers felt a close kinship with the animals. The animals would know that their two-legged relatives were calling them to come back.

Every day hunters walked afar, searching, always hoping to bring back something to eat.

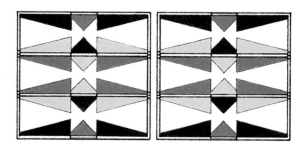

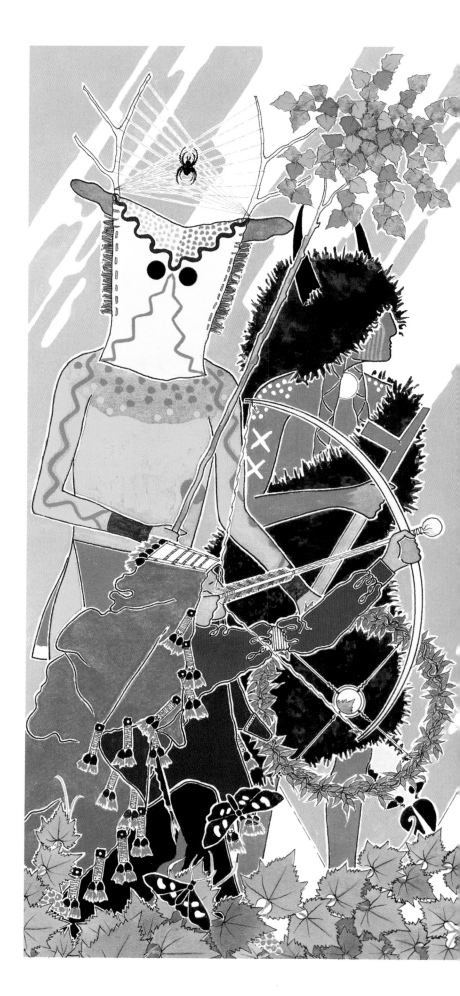

Finally, everyone was weak and without enough hope to take down the tipis and walk farther.

The leaders of the village chose two young men and told them:

"You, boys, are still strong. Most of us are weak or old, and you can hear the children always crying for something to eat. We now rely on your strength. You must find the buffaloes. Go to those high hills. Climb to the tops and look out over the country, and come back when you have found the buffaloes. Try hard! We all put our hopes in you."

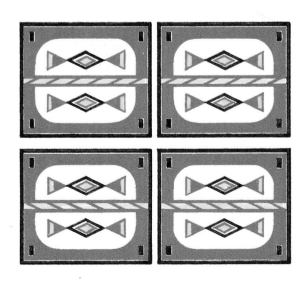

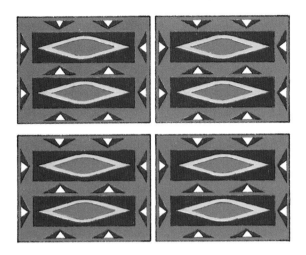

When the young men reached
the hills, they climbed up
through pine-tree forests,
and clambered up the rocks
at the very top.

They looked to the Four
Corners of the World. They
hoped to see the buffalo
herds making the plains
black with their numbers, but
they could not see even one.

"I think we will die
together here," one of the
scouts said. "These rocks
will mark our burying place.
They told us not to go home
until we found the buffaloes."

"You are right," the other
answered. "I did so want to
tell something good to make
my parents smile again."

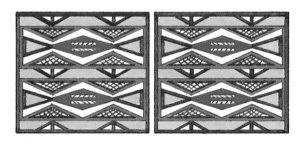

As they walked among the hilltops, suddenly they smelled buffaloes! They were amazed to find hoofprints everywhere around the entrance to a cave. While they puzzled, a voice said: "I will feed your people."

At a little distance stood a woman, mysterious and wonderful to look at. Her hair was tied with sage leaves and buffalo hair, and her dress was painted red in a manner they had never seen.

As they looked, they saw that the hill was really a tipi, and the cave its door.

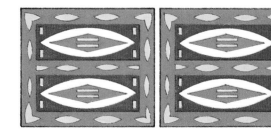

The woman led them inside, and sat them down on either side of her.

"Grandmother, our people are starving," they told her.

"Why have you not come sooner, Grandsons?" she asked. "Why have you gone hungry for so long?"

Suddenly she pointed, "Look this way!" and for an instant they glimpsed animals of every kind.

"Look over there!" she said, pointing in the opposite direction, and for a moment the tipi appeared black with stampeding buffaloes.

"I will give you all these, Grandsons," she told them. "I will feed your people, and make them happy. Tell them: I will send out my Buffalo People. Go now!"

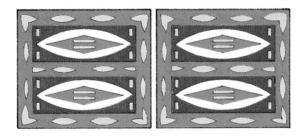

The young men ran down to the plains. Now they had marvelous words to take home: "I will feed your people, and make them happy," she had told them. They did not feel weak or hungry or tired any longer. When they came in sight of their village again, they started to sing and run a crooked course from side to side, which was the signal that they had something important to report.

Great was everyone's joy and excitement. "We will go and see this wonderful woman," the wise ones decided. "Let us each take her a gift."

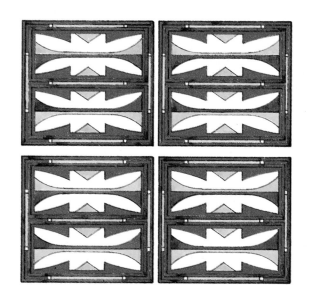

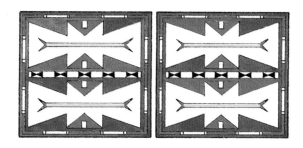

The two young men led the way up to the cave, and all the people climbed up after them. Those who were strong carried the children and helped the weaker ones.

On the ground at the entrance to the cave, women spread out beautiful buffalo robes which they had painted. People placed their gifts on the robes. Even the children gave their dolls or toys, and those who had none gave pretty stones or flowers.

They waited. Nobody spoke. Even the camp dogs sat quietly.

When the mysterious woman did not appear, they all walked back to their tipis.

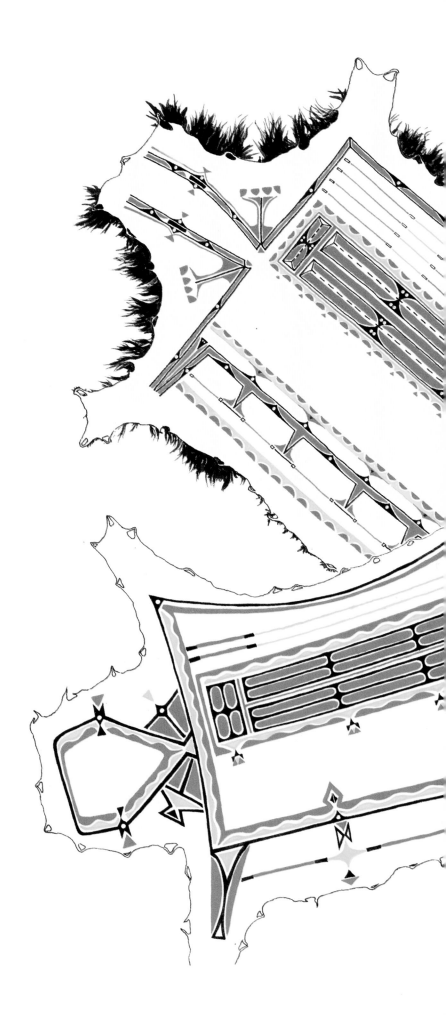

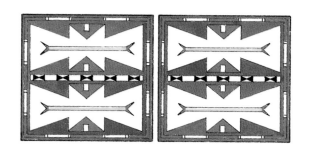

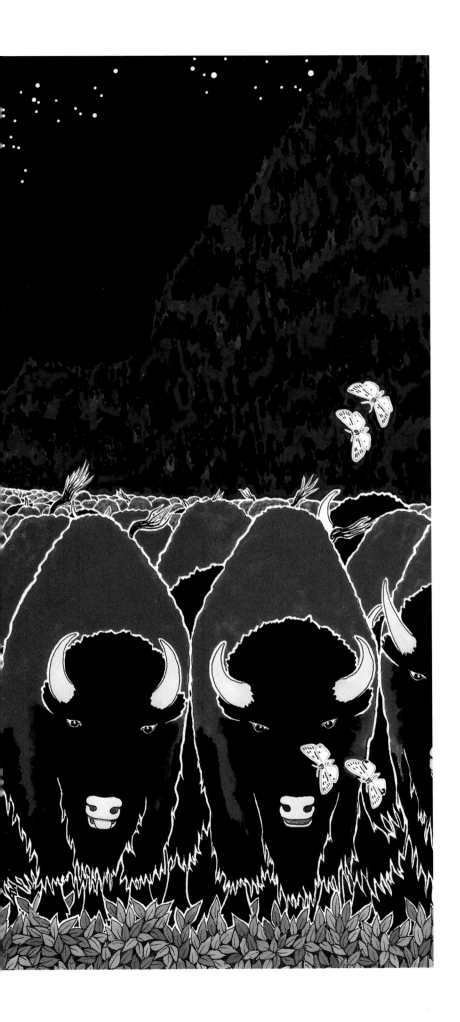

The sun went down, and again the children went to sleep without anything to eat.

And then, during the night everyone was awakened by a thunderstorm drumming and booming in the hills. When the sound grew louder, they rushed outside and hammered in the pegs around the bottoms of the tipis and closed the smoke flaps against the storm. Yet there was no lightning! Even no wind, and the sky was full of stars! The rumbling swelled to a terrifying roar and the ground under their feet trembled.

"It's the Buffalo Nation!" they cried. "The buffaloes are coming!"

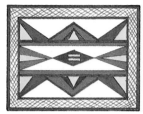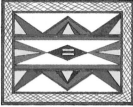

All through the night they
came out of the cave,
surging like a torrent down
from the hills and rushing
past the tipis. The air was
filled with noises of snorting
and bellowing and
thundering hooves.

People crouched inside
their tipis, hiding under their
robes. Mothers held their
children close, fearful that
the buffaloes would knock
down the tipis and trample
them in their frantic rush.
The huge beasts raced past,
crowding one upon another.
Those who were brave
enough to peep through
holes in the tipi covers
became dizzy watching the
multitudes hurrying by.

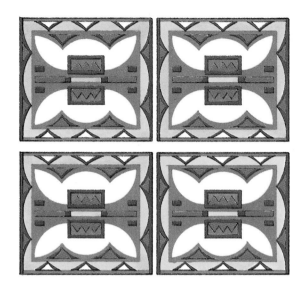

As the sun arose the tipi doors were thrown open. The wonderful woman had brought back the buffaloes. It was just as she had promised the young men.

After that the hunters went out and brought home meat. There was laughter again, and delicious cooking smells came from every tipi.

Wise men gave thanks for the food, and everyone had enough to eat. Even the dogs and magpies were happy.

Later they sliced the rest of the meat to dry in the sun, and the parfleches were filled once again.

That is the story the old people used to tell about those long-ago days. **Keyapi***, that is what they said.*

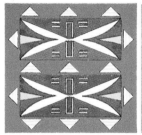
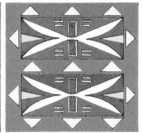

Today, National Park Rangers take tourists down into the caverns to look at the strange and beautiful rocks deep inside the earth. People hear the silence down there, and see the darkness.

Sometimes they feel an extraordinary wind inside the cave. People say this wind is the breath of yet more buffaloes, still somewhere down there, waiting for the mysterious and wonderful woman to let them out.

When a buffalo was killed, little of it was wasted. Various parts were eaten either raw, cooked, or sun-dried. The following is a list of some of the other uses:

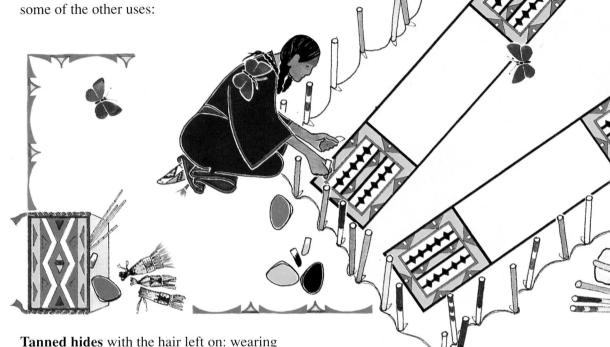

Tanned hides with the hair left on: wearing robes for winter; tipi floor covering; mattresses and bedding. Tanned hides with the hair removed: wearing robes for summer (calf skins for children); cradles; men's and women's leggings; tipi covers and lining; moccasin uppers; saddle blankets; pad saddles; quivers; many kinds of bags and pouches; gun cases; burial shrouds.

Rawhide, which is soft when wet, shrinks as it dries and becomes hard and very strong: parfleche containers and trunks of many kinds; shields to deflect arrows; knife scabbards; moccasin soles; ropes; lariats and saddles; stirrups; drumskins; rattles; glue; handle wrappings for war clubs and stone hammers to give strength and flexibility; bull boats, which were lightweight rounded rafts rather like modern rubber rafts.

Skull: altar.

Horns: cups, spoons, ladles and bowls; attached to headdress; bow construction; powder horns; arrow points; spinning tops.

Bones: awls; porcupine quillwork flatteners; arrowheads; knives; axes; porous rib-bone paint brushes; scrapers and tools used in tanning; sled runners; wood-shaping tools.

Hair: light ropes; bridles and halters; hair ornaments; stuffing for saddles, pillows, drumsticks, dolls, and balls; insulation in moccasins for winter.

Muscles and sinews: thread for sewing, in any thickness from the finest filaments for embroidery to heavy strands for sewing moccasins; bow strings and ropes; glued to bows to add strength; lashings and bindings used in fastening points and feathers to arrows.

Dung: often the only fuel on the plains, where few trees grow.